Henry's Song

For Eve & Alice K.C.
For Mum & Dad S.H.

Published by
Lion Publishing plc
Sandy Lane West, Oxford, England
www.lion-publishing.co.uk
ISBN 0 7459 4442 6

First hardback edition 1999
First paperback edition 2000
10 9 8 7 6 5 4 3 2 1 0

A catalogue record for this book is available
from the British Library

Typeset in 20/32 Baskerville MT Schoolbook
Printed and bound in Singapore

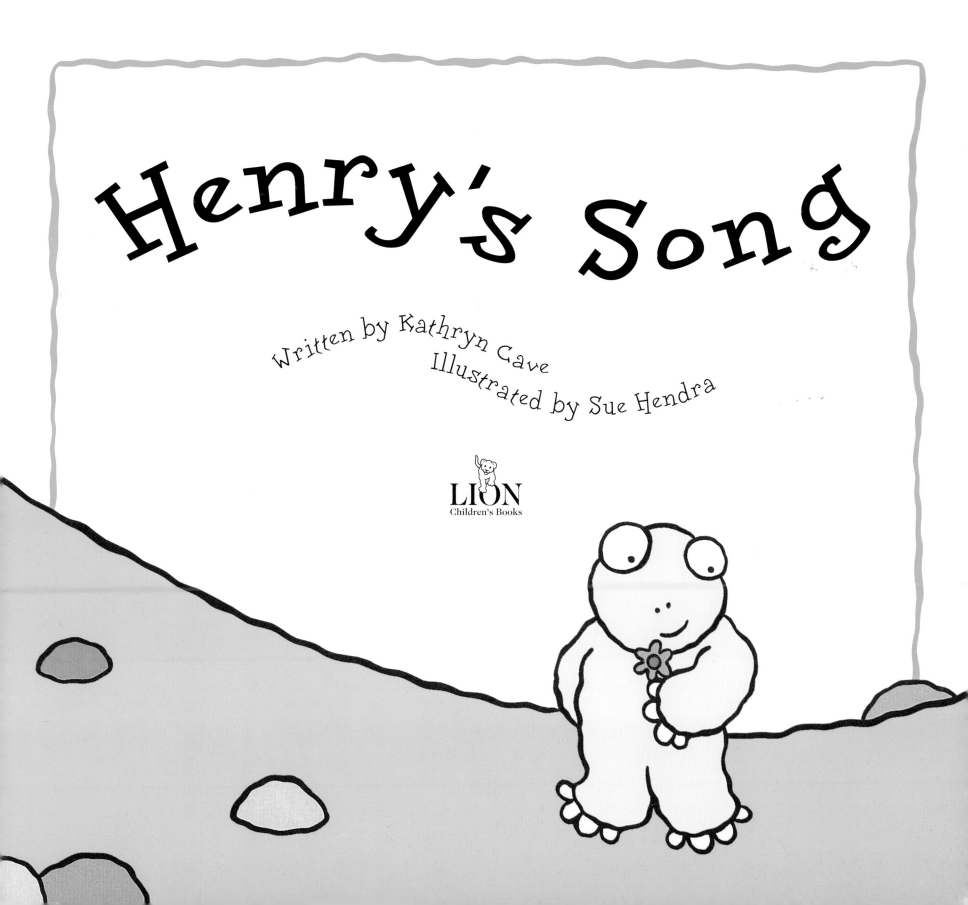

Henry's Song

Written by Kathryn Cave
Illustrated by Sue Hendra

LION
Children's Books

Early one morning, while the forest was still asleep,
Henry woke up. The sun had just risen.

The grass shone with dew.

It was a beautiful day to be alive.

Henry felt happy.

He did something he had never done before.

He took a deep breath and he sang.

The song was loud, and joyful, and full of surprises.

All at once, the forest woke up.

'What's that noise?' the creatures cried.

'Put a sock in it, Henry!'

Henry didn't hear them.

Soon there was snarling and shrieking,

shouting and cheeping,

trumpeting, cawing, growling and

ROARING all over the forest.

Suddenly, the bright sky grew dark.

'What's all this noise?' asked a voice like thunder.

The maker of all things had woken up.

The trees shook, the grass trembled,

and everyone became very quiet.

'Listen to me,' said the voice. 'I made you, and I made you well. I gave you legs to run, paws to dig, eyes to find food, mouths to eat it. I gave you ears so that you can hear me. Now tell me this: what are your voices for?'

None of the creatures said a word. Nobody knew the answer.

'Think about it,' said the voice. 'Tomorrow I will ask again.'

The grass shook, the trees trembled, and the maker of all things went back to sleep.

All morning the creatures argued about

how to answer the maker's question.

Their voices were all so different.

Some croaked, some cawed. Some cooed, some roared.

There was not one noise they could **all** make together.

What **were** their voices for?

At last someone said, 'This morning Henry's song put the maker in a bad mood. Tomorrow, let's sing a proper song, the most beautiful song the forest has ever heard.

Then the maker will be pleased, and there will be no more questions.'

Everyone stopped arguing, and shouted, 'YES!'

The creatures wanted their song to be perfect.

So they practised. They squashed and squeezed
themselves into a circle.

One by one they made their way to the centre
and lifted their own special voices.

When Henry's turn came, he clasped his paws,
he lifted his head, and he sang with all his heart.

Henry's song was very special.

The others might have liked it if they'd listened properly,

but they hadn't. They covered their ears and said, 'Call that

singing? We'll never please the maker with a noise like that!'

Then they said Henry couldn't join in their song for the maker.

He begged and pleaded, but they went on saying, 'NO!' until

the forest went to sleep.

Next morning, the creatures sang for the maker of all things.
It was a wonderful song, but something was missing, and the
hearer of all things knew what it was.

'Stop!' said a voice like thunder. 'Why can't I hear Henry?'

'I can't sing,' said Henry, hanging his head.

'Can't sing? But of course you can! That's what voices
are **for**!' cried the maker.

'To make your song perfect, you need to sing together.

Would you try that?' asked the maker gently.

'ALL of you? Every single one?'

So the creatures did.

'Join hands and join in.'

'This song's for everyone to sing!'

'That's PERFECT,' said
the maker of all things.
And it was.